Mrs Maginty
and the
Cornish Cat

written by
Ann Jungman

Illustrated by Leonie Shearing

1 Mrs Maginty and the Cornish Cat

Holidays! Everyone goes on about holidays as though they were the best. I hate holidays! That is, I used to, until last summer when something happened that made me realise that holidays really could be fantastic. And I mean fantastic! To be honest, when we set off, there was not even the smallest hint that it was *not* going to be like all our other family holidays – horrible. And I mean horrible!

In fact the holiday started like every other, with Dad putting all the bags in the boot and slamming it shut. Then off we went, like every other year, to pick up my gran and grandad. They always come with us, every single year. They never seem to enjoy it and I've never understood why they come, but they do. It's just one of those family things that happens for no good reason at all.

Now that I'm getting bigger there really isn't room for all of us in our car, so we travel down to Cornwall all squashed together and that makes everyone even more bad tempered than before.

Let me fill you in a bit.

Every year my parents, Graham and Jennifer Mason, rent a cottage in Cornwall. Every single year! All my friends go off to France and Spain and

Greece but we can't do that because of Grandad – I'll explain about that later. Now don't get me wrong. I love Cornwall, but a change would be nice. Anyway, the point is that Mum and Dad and I always go on holiday with Gran and Grandad.

Gran and Grandad are my dad's mum and dad and he's their only son. Grandad was in the Navy during the War and got injured, so he never managed to work again. I think he's in pain quite a lot of the time, which makes him a bit bad tempered. My gran is pretty sad too. Dad says she used to be loads of fun but that was before Grandad was injured.

My mum is great but she is always very quiet on these holidays. I think she'd much rather not go self-catering. She says it's more work than staying at home, but every year it's Cornwall and every year it's a cottage! You begin to get the picture? We were a family that just couldn't get on with each other. Either no one said anything or everyone talked at once and nobody listened.

This year was a specially difficult year because I had heard my dad saying to my mum one evening, when they thought I was in bed, 'Jenny we've got to talk. I've just been round at my parents and they can't manage any more. They'll have to move in with us.'

My heart sank. I knew I wouldn't be able to stand it at home with Gran and Grandad living with us.

'But Graham, we don't have the room,' said Mum.

'I know, but if we sell this house and they sell their flat, we could buy a bigger place and they could live on the ground floor.'

No way! I thought. I loved our house and didn't want to move and I knew Mum didn't either.

'But we've only been here a couple of years, Graham. We've just got the house the way we want it and the garden's looking lovely, Rosie is doing well at her school and we get on with the neighbours. I know I sound selfish but I don't want to move again.'

'I understand, darling, and I don't want to either, but my father is getting weaker and more demanding, and poor old Mother just isn't up to it, and we can't afford a full-time nurse.'

'I know,' sighed Mum, 'and I'm fond of your parents, I really am, but you know what it's like when we go on holiday. And that's only for two weeks! It wouldn't be fair on Rosie – you know how particular your father is. She'd have to be quiet all the time in her own home.'

'I know, I know,' groaned Dad, 'but I can't see any alternative. I'm their only child and they need help. If they ask, I will feel I have no choice but to say "yes".'

So with all that going on in the background, the future didn't look very rosy – to put it mildly. But that was before our super, special magic holiday.

To cut a long story short, we drove all day and arrived in Polperro just as it was beginning to get dark. All I can say about that journey is thank goodness for personal stereos or a murder would have been committed – probably by me.

Dad drew up outside a pretty stone cottage and got out of the car and slammed the door. A woman came out and handed Dad a key and pointed him towards a small lane. Dad got back into the car looking tired and fed up.

'I hope it's not much further dear,' Gran said to Dad. 'Your father's very hot and tired. This journey is too much for him. Next year I think we should come separately by train.'

'I did suggest that, Mother,' said Dad, sighing wearily. 'It's not much further now, about a mile up that lane.'

So we drove on. It was so beautiful that I forgot about being hot and tired.

We drove along the windy lane. It had thick hedgerows on either side and flowers in soft colours that gave off sweet scents. There were birds singing merrily in the trees, as if to welcome us. Just as I had decided that things couldn't get any more glorious I noticed that we were driving through orchards. On the right was an apple orchard laden with apples and there were other trees full of delicious, shiny, tempting red cherries.

Mum began to sing quietly. 'Cherry ripe, cherry ripe, fresh ones and fair ones.'

Then, to my absolute amazement, Dad joined in. 'Who will buy my cherries ripe?'

And then, you'll never believe this. Gran *and* Grandad began to sing too. I didn't know the words, I mean it's a pretty old-fashioned sort of song, but to my surprise I began to hum anyway. By the time we arrived at the cottage everyone was laughing and singing. A first for all of us, I can tell you! We got out of our car and looked at the cottage.

I've never seen a prettier house, it was like a picture on a postcard. It had stone walls and a thatched roof and the garden was full of hollyhocks and lupins, and flowers of every colour under the sun. Behind the cottage was a wood and behind the wood the sun was

going down. The sky was the most amazing shade of orange red. It was then that I noticed the front door of the cottage was open. My heart sank. We must have come to the wrong cottage and I so wanted this to be our holiday cottage!

'Look Mum,' I said, 'the door's open. We must have come to the wrong cottage.'

'No,' insisted Dad looking puzzled. 'It says "Avalon Cottage" on the key and look there above the front door.'

We all looked and there carved into the stone was written, 'AVALON COTTAGE, 1642'.

'Maybe there's been a mix-up,' suggested Gran. 'Maybe they've let the same cottage to two families. I hear about that sort of thing all the time. My neighbour went to Spain and the hotel they were booked to stay in hadn't even been built. It's all the same nowadays, no one cares.'

That was typical of her; always expecting the worst. I thought of living with it all the time and my heart sank.

'I'm going to sort this out,' said Mum briskly, and she took the key and walked up the path. Just as she was about to put the key in the door it was flung open.

There stood a smiling, pink-cheeked old lady with a mop of white hair done up neatly in a bun. 'There you all are,' she cried cheerfully. 'I was beginning to worry that you'd have to drive down that windy little lane in the dark. No fun if you're not used to it. Now come on in, I've just made a big pot of tea and some scones.'

'With raspberry jam and clotted cream?' I asked hopefully.

'Of course,' agreed the strange woman. 'This is Cornwall after all, so a Cornish cream tea is called for.'

'Have we got the right place?' asked Mum looking perplexed. 'We're the Mason family and we're booked for Avalon Cottage for two weeks starting today.'

'Of course you've got it right. Now, there I am forgetting my manners again. I'm Mrs Maginty and I come with the cottage. I do all the cooking, cleaning and shopping so that my guests can spend all their days just doing whatever they fancy: enjoying themselves, having a real holiday break.'

A look of huge relief flooded across Mum's face. 'Oh, well that sounds wonderful Mrs Maginty.'

'Now come on, in you come and have your tea. You all must be dead tired after your long drive. You go ahead,' Mrs Maginty told Gran. 'I'll help Mr Mason senior. I used to be a nurse.'

So we all sat at the large round table and tucked into tea and scones and jam and cream. It was without a shadow of doubt the best cream tea I had ever had.

'Look,' said Dad embarrassedly, as he downed his fourth cup of tea, 'I don't quite know how to say this but there must be some mistake. We didn't know there was going to be a housekeeper.

We only paid for the house. We can't afford to pay for you as well.'

'Oh bless you,' replied Mrs Maginty laughing. 'I don't cost anything extra. Now I'm here to see that you enjoy yourselves. So go and freshen up a bit and unpack. By the time you've done that I'll be ready to serve supper. I've got a tasty cottage pie in the oven and fresh beans from the garden and there are ripe cherries just picked from the orchard.'

Mum grinned from ear to ear. I haven't seen her look so happy for months. 'Oh Mrs Maginty,' she said, 'I can't tell you how wonderful it is to arrive and not to have to start cooking. I'm so glad you're here.'

Mrs Maginty beamed back. 'Up you go dear and have a nice hot bath before supper.'

The inside of the house was as beautiful as the outside: lots of small rooms with black beams and white walls. The furniture was simple and bright and the evening light streamed in through the latticed windows.

I went upstairs into one of the rooms. It looked out on to a beautiful view of the hills. Everything about this place seemed magical. I went over to the bed and flopped down and that's when I saw it – a pitch-black cat was spread out on the white pillow case. I stroked the cat, who woke and purred for a minute, before curling up and going to sleep again. I got changed by which time the most wonderful smells were wafting up the stairs.

I raced downstairs with the black cat at my heels. Then, in turn, the cat went and rubbed itself up against everyone's legs.

'Merlin, come here,' said Mrs Maginty gently, and the black cat went and sat down next to Mrs Maginty.

At supper, Mum, Dad, Gran and Grandad all got on unusually well and I started to think about Merlin, the cat. 'Was he a magic cat?' I wondered.

Then, when Mrs Maginty put a bowl of pudding in front of me, she bent down and whispered in my ear. 'Why don't we let this be our little secret dear? It will be easier that way.'

As I tucked in, I grinned and nodded my head in agreement. It was going to be fun to have a secret with Mrs Maginty. I began to feel that I was going to enjoy this holiday after all.

Why didn't Rosie usually enjoy her annual summer holiday?

Why do you think this holiday might be different?

2 Grandad

'Atishoo!'

I sat up in bed and gave the biggest sneeze ever. I looked round and saw Merlin at the end of the bed. I know that cats can't smile but I'd swear that one did. Merlin jumped elegantly off the bed and went and stood by the door.

'You want me to get up, don't you?' I said to Merlin. The cat purred and rubbed itself against the door. I felt it was saying, 'Certainly do.'

So I quickly got washed and dressed and followed Merlin downstairs. The delicious smell of frying bacon and sausages drifted up the stairs.

In the kitchen stood Mrs Maginty smiling away as she cooked breakfast. 'Good morning,' she cried, 'and isn't it a lovely day for your holidays? Now I've done bacon, egg, mushrooms and tomatoes for you. Now I expect you'd like a slice of fried bread as well.'

'It's my favourite,' I told her.

'I thought so,' smiled Mrs Maginty. 'I've got fruit and yoghurt for your mum because she's so fussy about her figure and two nice kippers for your gran and grandad.'

'How did you know that kippers were their favourite?' I demanded, my mouth full of egg and bacon.

'Oh I don't know, someone must have told me, I suppose.'

Soon the whole family were sitting round the kitchen table, all eating something different for breakfast but all having their favourite food.

Everyone seemed to be in a good mood. I began to think that this was definitely going to be a holiday with a difference.

Then there was a knock at the door and in walked a big man with a red beard wearing big boots and a striped sweater. You could see at a glance that he was a fisherman. 'Good morning all,' he said, 'Lovely day. Morning Mum,' he said to Mrs Maginty, giving her a kiss.

'This is my son, Percy,' she explained, 'Percy goes and gets all my shopping for me.'

'That's right,' said Percy, 'but I'm a fisherman by trade, got my own boat in the harbour. I sometimes take visitors out in it, so if any of you has a fancy to spend a few hours at sea, I'd be happy to take you.'

Then he turned to Grandad, who had his mouth full of kipper. 'I hear you used to be at sea yourself once, sir.'

'That's right,' replied Grandad. 'I was on a battleship during the war.'

'Then maybe you'd like to come out in my boat,' said Percy eagerly. 'I wouldn't charge you like, have it on the house.'

'My husband has never been in a boat since his ship was torpedoed during the war,' said Gran quickly. 'It's very kind of you but we will have to refuse.'

At that moment, Merlin the black cat walked across Grandad's shadow.

'Now that is a very handsome offer, Percy,' said Grandad, 'I think I will go. It's a lovely day and the sea's as flat as a mill pond. Can't think of anything I'd like better than a little sailing expedition.'

The whole family stared at Grandad in amazed silence. We all knew that ever since he had spent eight days lost at sea on a raft, Grandad had always insisted he would never get in a boat again.

'I'll just finish my cup of tea and then I'll be right with you, Percy.'

'Aye, aye captain,' said Percy smiling.

'You'll have a cup of tea yourself then, Percy?' asked Mrs Maginty, smiling fondly at her huge son.

As she poured the tea, Gran began to look worried and tearful. 'I can't believe you're going to do this, Arthur,' she said. 'You know how upset you become when you even think about what happened to you. You'll have nightmares tonight and I'll be the one who has to look after you.'

'I think it's a very good idea for Grandad to go for a short sail round the bay on such a calm day,' interrupted Mum, firmly. 'It might help him come to terms with what happened.'

'It's all well and good for you, Jennifer,' sniffed Gran. 'I have to deal with him when things go wrong.'

'All I was trying to say,' replied Mum, 'was that this is a chance and he should take it.'

I sighed. It was beginning to sound like all the other holidays with everyone arguing and getting angry.

'I think you're right about that, Mrs Mason,' said Mrs Maginty quietly. 'It's certainly worth a try.'

'I couldn't agree more,' said Grandad firmly. 'For the first time in over fifty years I feel able to go to sea again and on that very day, young Percy here walks in through the door. Now if that isn't a coincidence I don't know what is.'

I caught Mrs Maginty's eye and we smiled at each other.

'Well Arthur, if you insist, what can I do?' moaned Gran, getting that 'no one listens to me' look on her face. 'I'll go and get your warm sweater and your rubber boots, your pills and your inhaler.'

'Thank you Muriel, that would be very kind.'

While she was upstairs Dad said to Grandad, 'Are you sure this is a good idea, Dad? I mean it might bring on an attack.'

'Don't worry,' replied Grandad cheerfully, 'I feel sure I'll be able to cope with it. Maybe I can rid myself of those old nightmares. I mean they're over half a century old. Time for them to take off and say goodbye!'

Percy went off to get the boat ready and Dad got ready to drive Grandad down to the harbour. This I must see, I thought to myself, so I hopped into the back of the car. The harbour was the most super place with lots of little boats bobbing about on the water, while the sun made patterns on the waves. All around the jetty were little stone houses painted in pretty colours.

Dad and Percy helped Grandad into Percy's boat, *The Merry Knight*. As soon as Grandad was sitting down, Percy undid the rope that tied the boat to the jetty and away they sailed. I waved and jumped up and down. 'Have a great time, Grandad,' I yelled, keeping my fingers crossed on both hands.

As they sailed away sounds of laughter drifted back to us across the waves. Dad looked through his binoculars and grinned.

'What are you smiling at, Dad?' I asked.

He handed me the binoculars and I looked. There was Grandad steering the boat, with the wind blowing through his white hair and his face with an expression of peace and happiness that I had never seen. I gave a little sniff because I sort of wanted to cry. It was as though Grandad heard me, because he chose that moment to give a cheerful little wave.

'What a relief,' said Dad. 'He's having a great time. Now young Rosie, why don't I give you a tennis lesson before it gets too hot?'

Now that may sound ordinary to you but I have been trying to get my dad to play tennis with me for ever and he was always too busy and there he was actually offering! I think Dad worries a lot about his father, and seeing Grandad so happy made him feel more free or something. Anyway, I took Dad's arm and we walked back to the car feeling pretty pleased with life.

3 Gran

When we got back to the cottage, Dad got his tennis racket out of the car and then he looked dismayed. 'Oh no, Rosie, we haven't brought your tennis racket, we won't be able to have a game, after all.'

'Don't worry, Dad,' I said confidently, 'I'm sure there will be a tennis racket that's right for me somewhere in the cottage.'

'I doubt it,' groaned Dad.

'Under the stairs, dear,' came Mrs Maginty's voice.

'What's under the stairs?' asked Dad.

'Tennis rackets, in all sizes,' came the reply.

We looked and there on the top of the pile was a racket just my size.

'Found a racket and a box of tennis balls.'

'Wonderful,' cried Dad, 'what a piece of luck. I'll just tell the others that we're going. Jenny,' he called upstairs, 'I'm taking Rosie off for a tennis lesson. Is that all right with you?'

'Sure,' shouted Mum from the bath, 'I'll come and join you later.'

'Great,' replied Dad. 'We'll see you down at the courts.'

Dad works so hard we don't get much time together, in fact no time at all. So it was a real treat having him all to myself.

'It's a long time since we did something together, just the two of us, isn't it?' he commented.

'Yes,' I agreed, 'years.'

'I know,' sighed Dad. 'Even holidays seem too packed and there are too many people around.'

'Haven't you noticed that this holiday is a bit different?'

'Different?' frowned Dad.

'Yes, different. I mean look, here we are talking and Grandad's out having fun in a boat – it's different, isn't it? Now why do you think that is, Dad?'

'Don't know really,' said Dad thinking hard. 'Nice cottage, lovely weather and a bit of luck, I suppose.'

'Do you think that maybe it has something to do with Mrs Maginty?'

'Mrs Maginty?' exclaimed Dad. 'What an odd question. Well I suppose her doing all the shopping and cooking helps and she seems kind enough but other than that, no, not at all.'

After that I gave up. I could see that I was the only member of the family who had rumbled as to what was going on, and as long as everything continued to go so well, that was just fine with me.

The tennis was fun. It turned out that I had a natural talent and caught on quickly. By the time Mum joined us, I was really enjoying myself.

'Hi!' called Dad. 'Do you think I should go back to the house and keep my mother company?'

'Definitely not,' said Mum. 'She and Mrs Maginty are out in the garden having a wonderful time.'

'Isn't she worrying about Grandad?' I asked.

'Doesn't seem to be,' replied Mum. 'She carried on a bit at first and Mrs Maginty held her hand and made her a cup of tea and she seems to be very cheerful.'

Gran, cheerful? I thought. This I must see for myself.

Gran, as you have probably realised, is the most miserable person you ever met. Mum says I have to understand that she has had a very difficult life with Grandad being so ill. Still it gets me down when she moans and groans and doesn't seem to enjoy anything.

Dad and I played for a bit longer and then I said I was worn out.

'Go on back to the cottage,' said Mum, 'and have a shower. You've done very well. Here take this for an ice-cream. We'll see you later.'

I hurried back to the cottage and as I opened the front gate I could hear Gran talking to Mrs Maginty. Merlin was walking in circles round Gran's ankles.

'These hollyhocks really should be cut back more Mrs Maginty, if you don't mind my saying so. When they get too tall they snap in the wind.'

'Well thank you for telling me,' replied Mrs Maginty. 'I need someone to tell me what to do in the garden. I just don't seem to have green fingers like some people.'

'Oh, I do all the gardening at home,' Gran told Mrs Maginty. 'You see for almost all our married life Arthur has been unwell and I've had to do everything.'

'That must have been very hard dear.'

'It has been Mrs Maginty, very, very hard and most people don't seem to understand that. Still one thing I've always enjoyed is my garden. Though, to be honest, it looks as though we'll have to sell our house and move in with Graham and then I may not even have my own garden any more.'

'Oh, so you're planning to move in with your son, are you?'

'It's the only thing to do, Mrs Maginty. I'm getting too frail to look after Arthur on my own. I must admit that we're both very reluctant to do it.

I mean it wouldn't be fair on Graham and Jennifer and Rosie, but I don't see we have any choice.'

Mrs Maginty had one of those wise looks on her face and Merlin kept pacing backwards and forwards. Then Mrs Maginty looked at her watch. 'Oh dear, it's eleven o'clock, those scones will be just ready. Let's go in and have a cup of tea and some of my scones and maybe you've got some photos of your garden I could look at.'

Gran's face lit up. 'Well, I do have a few. Would you really like to see them?'

I stood by the gate wondering if I should let them see that I was there, when Mrs Maginty saw me.

'Hello Rosie,' she called. 'Come and join your Gran and me, we're just going to have a little something to eat.'

Those hot scones and Mrs Maginty's home-made jam were a treat. I stuffed my face I can tell you. Gran found the photos of her boring old garden and showed them to Mrs Maginty.

'Oh it's lovely, dear,' said Mrs Maginty, 'just look at that rockery and are those fruit trees, down at the bottom there?'

'Yes,' said Gran smiling broadly. 'We have fruit pies and crumble all summer long.'

'Yes,' I agreed, remembering our summer teas on Gran's lawn, 'and she makes the best plum jam in the world.'

'I didn't know you liked it,' said Gran in a surprised tone. 'You never said.'

I thought for a minute and then I realised that I had never told Gran that

I loved her apple tarts and the crumble that she made and that super jam.

'Well, I do like it,' I said, 'and I'm sorry I forgot to tell you.'

'Don't worry about it love,' said Gran and she put her arms around me and gave me a kiss. Mrs Maginty smiled broadly at us.

'So your gran's a great cook as well as a great gardener.'

'Oh I wouldn't say that,' smiled Gran, 'but I can do a few things.'

'Well I've got a few apples here,' commented Mrs Maginty. 'My daughter Elaine dropped them over. Why don't you show me how to make one of those apple tarts that young Rosie here seems to like so much? I've spent so much time chatting I'm behind in my chores, so a bit of help with tonight's dinner would be gratefully received.'

'I'd love to,' said Gran.

And then I heard myself saying, 'Can I help you Gran? I'd like to help and I can learn how to make a tart at the same time.'

Gran gave a great big smile. I thought what a lovely smile she had and then realised that she hardly ever smiled. I decided to get to know Gran better. Once the tart was in the oven, I suggested that we go down to the jetty to meet Grandad as he came off the boat. At the mention of Grandad the smile drained from her face. 'Oh I do hope he's all right,' she said in her usual worried tone.

'He'll be just fine,' said Mrs Maginty, as she walked into the kitchen with a pile of white sheets smelling of lavender. 'My Percy will have looked after him a treat, so don't you go worrying yourself.'

Gran seemed to believe Mrs Maginty because her face relaxed again. 'Come on Rosie, let's go and meet your grandfather and who knows, maybe we could pick up an ice-cream on the way.'

Gran and I had a really good talk on our walk to the harbour – another first time ever experience.

Gran and I stood looking out to sea and right in the distance we saw the fishing boat sailing towards the shore. We both waved and stood on the jetty watching the seagulls and the fishermen mending their nets.

Grandad was thrilled to find Gran and me sitting on the jetty. 'This is a lovely surprise,' he called out, as Percy tied the boat to the jetty. 'Two beautiful ladies waiting for me. I'll have to buy you both an ice-cream.'

To be honest my heart sank. This would be my third ice-cream in one morning *and* all those delicious scones. I managed to smile and look pleased.

Percy helped Grandad out of the boat.

'You had a good time didn't you, Arthur?' said Gran fondly, looking at his red cheeks and his windblown hair.

'I did,' said Grandad, 'I really did. I don't know why I took so long going back to the sea. I mean it wasn't the sea's fault, what happened to me years ago. War was the culprit, not the sea.'

'You look ten years younger, Grandad,' I told him and he really did.

'Do you want me to drive you back to the house?' asked Percy.

'Oh yes,' said Gran, 'He'll be needing a rest.'

'Not quite yet,' cried Grandad, 'I would like to spend a bit of time here with my two beauties, if that's all right with you?'

'No problem,' said Percy, with his big Maginty smile. 'I'll just go over and see

my brother Lance who runs *The Fisherman's Arms* pub over there. Maybe you'd like to have a spot of lunch – he does a good lunch does Ben – the best fish and chips in Cornwall. Anyway, you know where to find me when you're ready.'

You will not be surprised to learn that Grandad bought us a most wonderful lunch and that Lance turned out to be just as nice and friendly as Percy and his mother. I wondered how many more Magintys we would meet before our holiday was over.

4 Mum

This chapter is about my mum. Mum's great, she's the best, number one, the tops, but she's a worrier. Once I got the hang of what was happening at Avalon Cottage, I knew that Mrs Maginty would do something about it, so I just sat and watched and waited. I didn't have to wait long.

On the second morning at the cottage I got up early, before anyone else. I thought I'd have a scout around and explore the area. I went for a great walk up to the top of the hill behind the cottage – it really was a fantastic place.

There were wonderful views of the sea in one direction and rolling green fields and woods in the other. I sat on the top of the hill and thought how very lucky we had been this year. Then I looked down at our cottage. It looked so cosy and pretty nestling at the foot of the hill, surrounded by apple orchards and flowers. Then I noticed something, something that wasn't visible from inside the cottage. The house was set within a circle of trees – looking from above it was absolutely clear.

So that's what it is, I thought. We are in a circle of enchantment, a magic ring, a fairy place.

Then I remembered that the stories about King Arthur and the Knights of the Round Table had all taken place in Cornwall and that Tintagel Castle nearby might be the ruins of King Arthur's Camelot.

Ummm, I pondered, this is all beginning to make sense. There is some ancient magic in this wonderful place. I must get *The Sword and the Stone* and read it again, I said to myself. Then I realised that there would be copies in the cottage, of course there would be. And suddenly I felt so happy I leapt up and ran down the hill with a slight breeze blowing in my face. As I got near to the house I could smell bacon cooking.

It's perfect, I thought as I reached the cottage. It's the most perfect place in the world.

When I ran in the door Mum was in tears and talking to Mrs Maginty. 'Oh there you are darling,' she cried, 'I was so worried. You mustn't just go off and not leave a note. I was just about to call the police. I went into your room to bring you a cup of tea and you weren't there. I've been looking everywhere, I've been out in the garden calling and calling. Promise me you won't do that again.'

'Mum,' I said firmly, 'all I did was take a walk up to the top of the hill. It was a lovely morning and I wanted to see the view. Why do you always get so anxious about everything?'

Mrs Maginty was watching us with one eye, while she turned over those crispy bits of bacon and she had a kind of wise look on her face. 'Rosie's right,' she said in a calm voice. 'I've raised any number of children and one thing I've learned is that you can't watch them all the time.'

'But it's so dangerous out there,' said Mum drying her eyes. 'Anything can happen. Things have got worse since you had young children, Mrs Maginty.'

'That's true,' she replied, 'but I look at it like this. Awful things do happen, that's a fact, but only to a minority of children. It seems to me that if you want to give children confidence in themselves, well they've got to be allowed to go out there into the world and find out about it themselves.'

'That's all well and good,' said Mum beginning to look tearful again, 'but I do worry so.'

Mrs Maginty put down the big black frying pan and came over to Mum and put her arm around her. 'I'll tell you one thing dear, nothing untoward will happen to young Rosie here while she's staying at Avalon Cottage, that I can promise you.'

'She's right, Mum,' I said, 'only good things happen to you here, you must feel that too.'

As I was speaking, Merlin crossed the room, walked right past me, then in front of Mum and out through the front door. After that I knew there wouldn't be any problems with Mum, and there weren't…

After breakfast Mum and I went down to the beach and we had a great time. We ran into the sea and jumped up and down on the big ocean breakers. We held hands and leapt in the air together and then let the waves carry us on to the beach, laughing as the white foam broke over us. I am delighted to be able to tell you that Mum didn't once say, 'Be careful,' or 'You all right?'

On the way back to the cottage we went looking for crabs in rock pools. I jumped from rock to rock in my bare feet and Mum just let me get on with it. We found lots of crabs and had a good

time. As we walked back to the house for lunch, I looked up at Mum. She looked more relaxed and happy than I'd seen her for years.

As we walked contentedly back to Avalon Cottage, we passed a Bowls Club. We stopped for a minute to watch. Then someone waved to us.

'It's Mrs Maginty,' I cried, waving back enthusiastically. 'And just look who's with her,' gasped Mum.

And yes, there they were, Gran and
Grandad, playing bowls and having
such a good time they were too involved
even to notice us.

'Thank you Mrs Maginty, King
Arthur, Merlin the black cat and anyone
else who is helping with this magic,' I
muttered under my breath. 'Thank you,
thank you, thank you.'

What good things have happened to the family
since they came to the cottage?

5 Dad

No doubt you are beginning to wonder what changes happened to my dad and I am going to tell you about it.

With Dad the problem is that he works too hard and he doesn't seem able to leave it behind. I don't think he really likes going on holiday. He'd rather work fifty-two weeks of the year and only take Christmas Day off as a break.

When we left the house it didn't seem any different from any other year. Dad left messages about his work on his telephone answering machine and he took his mobile phone along. While they were packing to leave I heard Mum say, 'Oh Graham, you promised not to bring any work away with you.'

'I know darling,' sighed Dad, 'I tried to organise it so I wouldn't need to take stuff with me, but there are a couple of contracts outstanding that I have to sort out. I'm sorry.'

'There should be at least two weeks a year you can devote to your family without taking the firm along,' complained Mum. 'Rosie will be very disappointed, she hardly ever sees you these days.'

'I'm truly sorry,' said Dad, pushing his hands through his hair. 'I'll make a point of spending time with her.'

'I hope you do,' snapped Mum, 'or she'll grow up and you won't have got to know your own child, which would be a pity because she is very nice.'

'I promise I'll only deal with these two contracts and apart from that I'll just be a husband and a father...'

'...and son,' Mum pointed out. 'Your parents are always so disappointed when you just disappear and don't have any time for them. It's not fair on us or on them.'

'I know,' groaned Dad, 'I promise I'll try this year, I really will.'

Well to be honest, I didn't really believe him. I mean, I knew he'd try, but I thought that in the end he'd give in and write long letters and faxes and be on the phone all the time, and Mum would have to do all the driving and looking after Gran and Grandad and get all stressed out. But that was not how it turned out at all.

Of course Dad did bring his portable computer with him and the first thing he did at Avalon Cottage was set it up in the little study at the back of the house. I noticed it on my way to supper on that first evening because Merlin was curled up fast asleep on the computer.

Looking back I can see that it was an important sign. Anyway the long and the short of it is that Dad could not get that computer to work. Dad asked Mrs Maginty if she knew anyone who might be able to mend it.

'I certainly do,' she told him, 'I'll call my son Gareth, there's nothing he doesn't know about computers. He'll have it working in no time.'

Then Dad and I went off to play tennis and when we got back the computer had gone and it was only returned five minutes before we left to go back home.

Gareth told Dad, 'So sorry about the delay. I had trouble getting one of the parts.'

'I didn't miss it,' said Dad, 'I was having too much fun getting to know my daughter and my two lovely parents and my one lovely wife.'

We all beamed when we heard that: Mum and me, Gran and Grandad, Mrs Maginty and Gareth Maginty and even Merlin the cat.

Still, I'm running on too fast. Dad seemed to get the feel of Avalon Cottage pretty quickly, because on the second day there, the phone rang. We'd just got back from the beach and were arguing as to who should use the shower first when I picked up the phone. Of course it was for Dad. 'It's the office,' I said sourly.

'Tell them I'm out,' yelled Dad as he raced up the stairs. 'And tell them I'll be out solidly for the rest of the next two weeks. Tell them to manage without me. I need a complete break and that's what I intend to have,' and the bathroom door slammed.

'I heard that,' said Dad's secretary. 'Tell him we'll see him in two weeks, to enjoy his holiday and not to worry, we'll be just fine without him.'

The next thing that happened to Dad was that the batteries on his portable phone ran down and wouldn't recharge. That did not come as a surprise to me because I saw Merlin fast asleep on top of the phone and by now I'd worked out what that meant. I suppose Mrs Maginty was worried that Dad might change his mind about not talking to the office.

Of course Gareth Maginty came and took the phone away and you will not be surprised to learn that it did not come back until the day we left. More spare parts shortages, I don't think!

By now, of course, you will have guessed what happened next. Dad had the best holiday of his life. Work and the office didn't get even one single mention for the rest of the time we were away. Every day Dad was just there for us and we did lovely things like walking along the beach, playing tennis, having picnics, eating out, and even water-skiing. Dad went fishing with Grandad and took Gran out to lunch and to listen to the band play on the front. None of us could remember seeing him quite so relaxed before. A couple of days before the holiday was due to end, Dad and I went blackberrying together and Dad said, 'What a splendid holiday this has been. I don't remember when I last had such a good time.

Now is there anything special you would like to do before we go home?'

'I'd like to go to King Arthur's castle in Tintagel,' I told him.

'Good idea,' said Dad, 'I always enjoyed the stories of King Arthur and the Knights of the Round Table. Grandad always loved them too, I think that's why he was called Arthur.'

'What do you mean?' I asked. This was getting very interesting.

'I think your grandfather was called Arthur after King Arthur. His father was called Arthur too. It's a kind of family tradition.'

'Then why weren't you called Arthur?' I asked.

'I was,' said Dad. 'Arthur Graham, but I hated it, it was so old fashioned, so I always used my second name,' and he stuffed a handful of berries into his mouth. 'Well if we're going to Tintagel, we'd better get a move on. Let's go and see who else wants to visit the castle.'

It turned out that they all wanted to come, even Gran and Grandad who'd been out doing their own thing every other day. 'You might find it a bit hard going,' Dad said to Grandad.

'I'll be fine,' replied Grandad. 'I'll take two walking sticks but I feel so much better I hardly know myself and I've got a special reason for wanting to visit Tintagel.'

'What's that Grandad?' I asked.

'Well a certain sailor took his gorgeous bride there on their honeymoon,' said Grandad, looking lovingly at Gran. Gran blushed but looked thrilled.

'We only had a week and we chose to come to Cornwall, partly because we both loved the old stories about King Arthur. It was a wonderful week,' she said enthusiastically.

'Yes,' agreed Grandad. 'We walked and swam and danced, it seems like yesterday. That was the only real holiday we ever had…'

'Until now, Arthur,' interrupted Gran. 'This has been a real holiday.'

'Yes, my love,' agreed Grandad, 'it certainly has.'

So we all went off to Tintagel and looked at the ruins of that grey and mysterious castle, perched high up on the towering cliff. There wasn't much to see, just some grey stones and a few arches on a green slope with the sea crashing on to the rocks below, but I felt the same sweet happiness there that I felt at Avalon Cottage.

Suddenly I looked around and
thought I saw a strange figure, standing
by a pillar. It looked like a knight in
shining armour but the sun was very
bright and when I looked again, there
was no sign of him. I stared at the space
he had occupied for a minute or two
and then looked down on the others.
They were all looking at the ruins.

That evening Dad and I took a walk to the top of the hill behind the cottage and watched the sunset. I pointed out the circle of trees.

'We're in a magic ring,' I told him.

Dad laughed. 'You always were a fanciful child Rosie, a magic ring indeed.'

'Dad,' I said after a few minutes, 'would you describe Grandad as a knight?'

'As a knight? Whatever are you on about, Rosie?'

'A knight, like in the stories about King Arthur?'

'You've had too much sun, early bed for you, my girl.'

'No, seriously Dad.'

'Well I suppose he was very brave, he volunteered to go on a particularly dangerous and important mission.'

'Yes,' I said. 'And what else?'

'I don't know. Really, Rosie, you ask the oddest questions.'

'Think, Dad.'

'Well, he gave up his place in the

lifeboat to wounded men. He's always kind and polite and tries to help. He cares about what is right and what is wrong.'

'And he's often in a lot of pain but he doesn't complain much,' I added.

'Yes, yes, that's right,' agreed my father thoughtfully. 'Yes, I suppose he is a modern kind of a knight. I mean he's not the kind of man who likes to fight but he thought the last war was a battle between good and evil and so he volunteered to join the Navy. My dad, a knight, what a strange idea. I never thought about it before.'

After that I felt I was getting a better understanding of why we were all in Avalon Cottage and why Mrs Maginty was looking after us.

What has made Rosie think her grandad is a 'modern day knight'?

6 Me

For the whole two weeks the weather was brilliant – lovely hot days and blue skies, with just the hint of a breeze. We spent most days outside doing holiday things and Mum and Dad went out for cosy dinners by themselves some nights. Gran and Grandad went off some evenings too, but when they stayed in they sat together and watched television and read. Most evenings I noticed they were holding hands.

Something tells me that you are all

waiting to hear what happened when Merlin crossed my path.

Well it didn't happen until the very last evening. I'd given up actually expecting it to happen. After all I'd got almost everything I wanted. Mum stopped worrying and began to enjoy herself. Dad had begun to realise that there was more to life than work and had begun to enjoy himself and enjoy us too. Grandad had stopped being afraid of the sea and had stopped having nightmares and seemed ten years younger, and Gran had stopped being a martyr and had started to do things she liked and seemed twenty years younger.

Then, on our very last evening, Merlin came and sat on my lap and gave me a knowing look. I thought he was just sharing the joke and thought nothing more of it. We had just had one of Mrs Maginty's wonderful suppers and were sitting back enjoying the sunset, when Grandad said, 'Muriel and I have been thinking hard about our future and we have something to tell you.'

My heart sank. They're going to spoil it by announcing that they want to come and live with us, I thought miserably.

'We've decided that we can't manage on our own any more and that we are going to sell our house,' said Gran.

'We both felt that as we were having such a good time here in Cornwall,' continued Grandad, 'that we would go and look at sheltered housing down here. It turns out that Mrs Maginty's heard of a lovely complex just a few miles from here.'

'Yes,' said Gran smiling, 'and would you believe it there is a little cottage that's just become available?'

I grinned. Yes, I'd believe it, I thought.

'But Mum' said my father, 'you'll be so far away from us. Are you sure you wouldn't rather be nearer London?'

'We thought about it dear,' said Gran, 'but the air down here is so good and with Mrs Maginty so near, we feel like we've got another family in Cornwall.'

'And there are two spare bedrooms in the cottage,' agreed Grandad, 'so any of our family who wants to come down will be very welcome.'

Whoopee, I thought, now we won't have to sell our house.

That night I lay in bed and I just couldn't sleep. I think we were all feeling very sad that our perfect holiday was coming to an end. There had been rather a flat atmosphere as we packed up the car ready to leave the next day.

Mrs Maginty had cooked us a very special meal and the whole Maginty clan had turned up for coffee and to say goodbye. I think we all felt a bit weepy that night. I just lay there for a while and then I felt an overwhelming urge to climb up to the top of the hill and look down on the cottage at night. So I got dressed quickly and crept out of the house.

Climbing the hill in the dark was lovely. The moon seemed to light up the sky like a beacon. When I got to the top, I looked down on the cottage and I could see the circle of trees making a faint black circle. As I stood there I felt a presence at my side. I looked up and there stood the knight I had seen at Tintagel. So I really had seen him after all. We stood together on the hillside and looked down at the cottage and the sea.

'This is an enchanted place, isn't it?'

'Aye maiden, that it is,' he replied.

'Why am I the only one in my family who knows that?' I asked. 'It seems so obvious.'

'In the world you live in, people know little of magic,' he answered. 'Only children retain some knowledge of it, hence you are the only one who understands what has happened here.'

'Will we go on liking and understanding each other?' I asked desperately. 'Will it go back to being like it was before we came here?'

'Things never go back,' he said with a sigh. 'Once people are touched by the magic and see things and themselves in a different way, they never return to their old ways. Fear not, your kinsfolk may not understand why things have changed, but they do know deep in their soul, that their old ways were bad.'

'Should I tell them what I know?' I asked him.

'Nay maiden, do not I pray you. They would not believe your words. Let these things be a secret between us for ever.'

'We'll be back next year. Will you be here then?'

'Aye, I will be here but you will not. I do not think that you will return to this place, and if you do, you will be older and less wise. You will not see me because you will have stopped believing.'

'Who are you?' I asked him. 'Were you one of King Arthur's knights?'

'I was,' he told me with his sad smile.

'And you wanted to help Grandad, that's why we came here, isn't it?'

'It is, maiden, he was a valiant knight, he needed my protection.'

'And you guard this place?'

'I do. This was always a place of good magic and I protect it for all of time.'

'And Mrs Maginty?'

'The lovely Gwen and I work together.'

'Gwen? Is that her name?'

'Aye – short for Gweniviere.'

'And Merlin?'

He laughed quietly. 'Yes, and the cat.'

'Was your name Maginty once, long, long ago?'

'You ask too many questions, Lady Rosemary. Now return to the house and try to remember this place and everything that's happened, and do good in the world.'

'Thank you for helping us and particularly for helping Grandad.'

The smile flickered across his face in the moonlight. He lifted his sword in that gesture that was a mixture of a salute and a blessing and faded away.

I walked back to the house feeling very peaceful.

I got back into bed. I fell asleep and slept like a log.

What has Rosie learned from the knight?

Do you think the family will go back to their old ways when they get home?

7 Us

Well, all good things come to an end, and this magnificent holiday was no exception. I could hardly bear the thought of leaving the cottage and Mrs Maginty and the knight and our very special enchanted place. The others weren't as miserable as me.

'We'll come back next year Rosie, I promise,' said Dad putting his arm around me.

'And we won't be far away Rosie.

When you come and see us, you can nip over and see Mrs Maginty as often as you want,' Gran told me.

'Yes darling,' added Mum, 'this isn't goodbye, it's au revoir.'

I knew they all believed what they were saying, but I knew, I just knew that it wasn't true. This would be our one and only visit to Avalon Cottage. Merlin came and sat on my lap and I began to feel better.

On our last morning Mrs Maginty made us the best breakfast ever.

'You've got a long drive ahead of you,' she said beaming at us.

Merlin sat next to me on the table and purred so loudly, that I knew it was his way of saying 'goodbye'.

After breakfast the whole Maginty clan came round to say goodbye. I cried a little bit and even Gran was dabbing her eyes with a hankie. Finally the goodbyes were over and we had to drive off. I leaned out of the car and waved until we rounded a bend and the Magintys and Avalon Cottage were out of view.

As we got close to the house where we had to hand in the keys, I began to feel a bit panicky – just suppose that as soon as we were outside the magic circle everything went back to what it had been before.

'Please don't let it be like that,' I prayed. 'Please let us hang on to all our new good, positive feelings.'

Mum jumped out of the car and went to hand in the keys.

'Did you have a nice holiday?' asked the woman in a tired voice. It was obvious she had asked that question so often, she hardly listened to the answer.

'Fantastic,' replied Mum enthusiastically. 'Just wonderful, and all thanks to your wonderful Mrs Maginty.'

'Mrs who?' demanded the woman frowning.

'Maginty,' said Mum in a surprised voice, 'The housekeeper and cook at Avalon Cottage, the one with the black cat, she said she came with the cottage.'

'No one came with the cottage,' snapped the woman. 'It's self-catering and I've never heard of a Mrs Maginty.'

'Everything all right?' asked Dad, as a rather dazed Mum climbed back into the car.

'She says she's never heard of Mrs Maginty and that she certainly didn't come with the cottage.'

'Very odd,' agreed Dad, as the car pulled away.

'I expect the woman's new and doesn't really know about it,' suggested Gran.

'Yes,' nodded Grandad, 'that's what it will be.'

Grown-ups honestly – talk about stupid!

You're probably wondering what happened to us on the return journey and when we got back to London, and

I'm glad to assure you that this story has a happy ending. Well, almost a happy ending.

As we got further from Avalon Cottage, I looked round at everyone for signs of backsliding but no, they went on looking relaxed and cheerful.

Well we're just on our way back from a wonderful holiday, I thought, maybe it will all wear off once we get back to everyday life.

But it didn't. Dad came home one day and announced what he had told the boss. 'I will only work the hours that I am paid to work, I have a wonderful family and I've missed too much of my child growing up and I'm not prepared to miss any more.'

Apparently the boss was a bit shocked but survived and Dad was always home by six o'clock and we never got work calls at home. Gran and Grandad sold their house and went to live in sheltered housing on the coast – although not actually the place they saw in Cornwall.

'We decided Cornwall was a bit too far from all of you,' Grandad explained.

'Yes,' agreed Gran, 'just as we've all got to like each other it seemed a good idea to be where you could visit us easily. We've found a place in Rye that is just beautiful.'

'Lovely,' agreed Grandad. 'Full of old sea dogs like me.'

'You're absolutely sure this is what you want, Father?' asked Dad.

'Oh definitely, but I'd never have taken the step if it hadn't been for that Cornish holiday.'

'You'll come and see us a lot, won't you?' said Gran in a worried voice.

I suddenly felt all weepy. They were my Gran and Grandad and they were going away. I gave them a hug. 'Just try and keep us away,' I said.

'We'll be down, Mother,' said Dad, 'don't you worry, Rye's a lovely place and not too far.'

And we did visit them often and it was always great.

As for Mum, she went back to

university to do a higher degree and did brilliantly and then went and got just the kind of job she deserved.

So you see, nothing was ever the same after that holiday. As for me, well I was very happy almost all of the time. I just loved my family and wouldn't have swopped them for anything. I also made a vow to myself. When I grow up, I will still believe in magic and knights and cats that smile. I will try to hang on to all of that; I will try very, very hard.

Of course we never did go back to Avalon Cottage. In fact we all just got on with our lives, but although we never went back, Avalon Cottage never really left us and as I grew older I realised that was just as it ought to be.

What does it mean when it says 'Avalon Cottage never really left us'?